THE GREATEST ADVENTURES IN THE WORLD

ALI BABA
and the
STOLEN TREASURE

TONY BRADMAN & TONY ROSS

ORCHARD BOOKS

ORCHARD BOOKS
96 Leonard Street, London EC2A 4XD
Orchard Books Australia
32/45-51 Huntley Street, Alexandria, NSW 2015
ISBN 1 84362 467 2 (hardback)
ISBN 1 84362 473 7 (paperback)
The text was first published in Great Britain in the form of a gift collection called
Swords, Sorcerers and Superheroes with full colour illustrations by Tony Ross, in 2003
This edition first published in hardback in 2004
First paperback publication in 2005
Text © Tony Bradman 2003
Illustrations © Tony Ross 2004
The rights of Tony Bradman to be identified as the author and of Tony Ross
to be identified as the illustrator of this work have been asserted by them
in accordance with the Copyright, Designs and Patents Act, 1988.
A CIP catalogue record for this book is available from the British Library.
1 3 5 7 9 10 8 6 4 2 (hardback)
1 3 5 7 9 10 8 6 4 2 (paperback)
Printed in Great Britain
www.wattspublishing.co.uk

CONTENTS

CHAPTER ONE
KASSIM AND ALI BABA   5

CHAPTER TWO
OPEN SESAME   11

CHAPTER THREE
KASSIM AND THE CAVE   23

CHAPTER FOUR
MARJANAH AND THE JARS OF   37
OLIVE OIL

NOTES ON THE STORY OF ALI BABA   46
A TALE OF GREED VERSUS
GOODNESS

KASSIM AND ALI BABA

IT'S A STRANGE FACT, BUT sometimes brothers can be so different from each other in character, you might think they couldn't possibly be from the same family at all.

Such was the case with two Persian brothers called Kassim and Ali Baba.

To put things in a nutshell, Kassim was as greedy, deceitful and arrogant as Ali Baba was generous, honest and good-hearted. Kassim married the daughter of a rich man to get at her father's money when he died; Ali Baba married a girl from a poor family for the simple reason that he loved her. So the two brothers seemed destined to follow very different paths.

Kassim did indeed grow richer and richer, but he always wanted more.

Ali Baba, meanwhile, barely made a living as a woodcutter, but at least he was happy with what he had. He was even happier when he and his wife had a baby son, although things were already tough for them, and it's harder to feed three mouths than two.

Still, the years went by, and Ali Baba and his family survived and stayed happy, and their baby son – who was called Ahmed – grew into a fine young man.

Then one day, Ali Baba set out as usual
for the forest with his donkey, and decided
to try his luck in a thicket he rarely
visited. He started work,
cutting branches, when
suddenly he heard
galloping horses,
and they were
coming his way.
Ali Baba
could hear the
unmistakeable chink
of weapons as well, and
that made him nervous. So
he pushed his donkey into the
undergrowth, and scrambled up the
nearest tree as quickly as he could.

He reached the top and looked down just as a column of forty horsemen appeared on the forest path. They rode past, and stopped at a wall of rock that stood beyond the thicket.

One glance at their wild, brutal faces told Ali Baba they were bandits. He quivered with fright.

CHAPTER TWO

OPEN SESAME

ALI BABA SAT IN THE TREE, trembling with fear, trying to stay concealed and hoping the bandits wouldn't notice the leaves shaking. But then something happened that made Ali

Baba stop trembling and his mouth fall open with wonder. One of the bandits – a very cruel-looking man who was obviously their captain, thought Ali Baba – dismounted and stood by the wall of rock.

"OPEN SESAME!" the captain said in a loud, strong voice.

And suddenly a hidden door opened in the rock, revealing a secret cave. The captain strode in, and his men dismounted

and followed him. Each bandit was carrying a bulging saddlebag. Ali Baba heard the captain say, "CLOSE SESAME!" from inside the cave, and the hidden door instantly swung shut.

Well, Ali Baba sat in the tree, amazed by what he'd seen and surprised that the name of a common seed could be magical. He wondered what on earth was going to happen next.

Then the door opened again. The forty
bandits emerged – their saddlebags
empty – and climbed back on their horses.
The captain said, "CLOSE SESAME!"
and the door swung shut, and the robber
band galloped away.

Ali Baba waited a good long while before
he climbed down from the tree,
to be sure that the bandits had
actually gone. But he did at
last, creeping up to the
wall of rock to examine
it – and there was no
sign of a door at all.
Ali Baba stood there
scratching his head, deeply
curious about what might be inside.

Then he wondered if the captain's words might work for him too...

"Open sesame," he whispered, far too nervous to say it as loudly as the captain of the bandits. But the door opened in just the same way as before.

Ali Baba cautiously stepped over the threshold of the cave. The bandits had left a torch burning in a wall sconce, and in its flickering light Ali Baba saw that the cave was much, much bigger than he'd thought – and that its floor was entirely covered in treasure!

Ali Baba thought bandits must have been storing their ill-gotten gains there for years.

Then he suddenly realised something else – this was a golden opportunity!

Ali Baba grabbed a couple of big bags of gold – the bandits wouldn't miss them from such a vast store, he thought – and hurried out of the cave, remembering to say, "Close Sesame!" as he emerged. The hidden door swung shut, leaving the wall smooth.

Then he loaded the bags of gold onto his donkey and headed for home.

Ali Baba's wife Ayesha couldn't believe
her eyes when he opened one of
the bags. Now it was her turn
to sit with eyes wide and
mouth open as Ali Baba
explained where the bags
of gold had come from.
Then she danced
around the room and
hugged her husband.
"How much have
we actually got?"
Ayesha said at last.
"I'm not really sure," said
Ali Baba, "and we don't
have time to count it. I want
to hide it as quickly as possible.

If somebody should see that we've got all this gold they might start asking questions. I think we should keep it a secret."

Ali Baba got Ayesha to help him hide the gold, then went out to sell his firewood as usual. Ayesha, however, couldn't rest until she knew the exact amount of their new-found wealth...and then she had an idea. She wouldn't have time to get the gold out of its hiding place, count it and hide it again before Ali Baba came home. But she would have plenty of time to weigh it.

Being a poor family, they had never had enough money to spend on luxuries such as a set of kitchen scales. Ayesha knew her sister-in-law had some though.

So she dashed off to Kassim's house.

"Kitchen scales?" said Kassim's wife Fatimah, who was as greedy and arrogant as her husband, and had a suspicious mind as well. "Of course I'll lend them to you, my dear. So long as you tell me why you need them."

"Oh, er…no special reason," spluttered Ayesha, who was too honest to feel comfortable telling lies. "I just have to weigh something, that's all."

"Is that so?" said Fatimah, smiling at Ayesha while her mind worked overtime. "Well, you wait here while I fetch them."

Fatimah went off to the kitchen and got out her scales. She carefully rubbed a little fat on the bottom of one of the pans. Then Fatimah re-joined Ayesha and handed over the scales.

Ayesha went home, quickly got out the gold, weighed it and hid it again. Then she returned the scales to her sister-in-law. She was too happy and excited to notice that one small gold coin had stuck to the fat in the pan. However, Eagle-eyed Fatimah soon found it...

That evening, Kassim went to see his brother. As soon as Ali Baba opened the door, his heart sank.

"So, it seems you've come into such a great sum of money, brother," said Kassim, scowling, "that your wife has to weigh it, and can afford to leave coins stuck to the pan." Ayesha squeaked. "You'd better tell me what's been going on," said Kassim.

Ali Baba sighed. But he couldn't be cross with his wife. He willingly told his brother the whole story.

Kassim's eyes glittered with greed. He went home, determined to take all the treasure of the cave for himself.

"Oh well, never mind," said Ali Baba when Kassim had left. "I'd been thinking we should use the money anyway. Who'll notice if we buy a few new clothes for ourselves? We could even hire a servant girl to help with the housework…"

So the next morning, Ali Baba, Ayesha and Ahmed went shopping in the bazaar. Then they hired a girl called Marjanah to be their servant. Marjanah was an orphan, and was very grateful for the job.

Meanwhile, an eager and excited Kassim was making his way through the forest with a train of donkeys to carry the hidden treasure home.

CHAPTER THREE

KASSIM AND THE CAVE

KASSIM ARRIVED AT THE
bandits' cave at last, and stood before
the wall. He looked round to make sure
he was completely alone, and cleared his
throat. Then he said, "Open sesame!"

And the hidden door opened smoothly, just as it had done for Ali Baba.

Kassim gave a little giggle of delight, and went into the cave. He lit a torch he'd brought, and stared at the kind of sight guaranteed to make the heart of a greedy man beat faster. But there was no time to waste. He said, "Close sesame!" and started choosing what to take. He soon had a great heap of bags and chests by the entrance, while his mind was fizzing with plans to return for the rest, and schemes for what he could do now he was probably the richest man in the world. He turned to face the door – and realised he had forgotten the magic words.

The truth was that Kassim's brain didn't have a great deal of room in it, and all the plans and schemes had pushed almost everything else out. He knew the first magic word was, "Open…" of course, that was obvious. And the second was a common seed, something you planted…

"Open…wheat!" he said, to no effect. "OPEN…CORN!" he shouted.

"OPEN…BARLEY! OPEN…RICE! Er… OPEN…OH, FOR HEAVEN'S SAKE, JUST OPEN!" But the door stayed obstinately, infuriatingly shut.

Kassim pounded on the rock with his fists – and suddenly it opened! But his smile of relief soon vanished…for standing outside were the forty thieves, their captain at their head. None of them looked too happy.

The captain drew out his sword – it was a great, curved, wickedly sharp scimitar – and advanced into the cave, pushing Kassim in too. Kassim stumbled, and fell…

The bandits were furious to discover
someone in their secret cave, and they
didn't stop to ask questions. The
captain killed Kassim, and
chopped his body into
several pieces, which
his men hung inside
the entrance as a
grisly warning.

Then they closed the
cave door and galloped
off down the forest path.

Night came, and Fatimah waited
for her husband to return. But the
hours passed with no sign of Kassim,
and by the time the sun rose the next
morning, Fatimah was frantic with worry.

She ran to Ali Baba's house, and demanded that he go and find out what had happened.

Ali Baba set off with his donkey, filled with fear for his brother. And of course, he was horrified when the cave door opened and he saw Kassim in pieces. He put the pieces into a couple of sacks, loaded them on the donkey, and then he hurried home to Ayesha and Fatimah with the terrible news.

Fatimah wailed and tore her hair, and Ayesha tried to comfort her. Ali Baba, however, was brooding about the consequences of Kassim's death.

"We can't let anyone know he was chopped up," he said. "If the bandits hear, they'll be able to work out that I know about the secret cave, too. We'll just have to find some way of putting Kassim's body back together again before we let the undertakers see him."

"Can I make a suggestion?" said somebody. It was Marjanah, the servant girl. She had already grown to love her kind employers – and she wanted to help them now.

"An old tailor lives on the other side of town," she went on, "and everyone says he's so good at his work that he could stitch a gash in your skin and leave no scar. Perhaps we could ask him to do it."

Ali Baba was impressed by Marjanah's cleverness, and so was Ahmed, who had come when he'd heard Fatimah wailing. In fact, the two young people rather liked the look of each other.

Marjanah went to see the tailor, and offered him a large payment for a special job.

He agreed, and Marjanah led him blindfolded to the dark cellar of Ali Baba's house, where she took off his blindfold and showed him the pieces of Kassim. The tailor shrugged, thought of the money, and did the job.

Then the tailor was blindfolded again and taken back to his shop, where Marjanah thanked him, gave him a large bonus, and swore him to secrecy.

Marjanah had been right – the tailor's work was so good you couldn't see the stitches.

The next day, Ali Baba
sadly announced that
his beloved brother Kassim
had died in his sleep, and an
expensive funeral was arranged.
And afterwards, Ali Baba sighed with
relief, and hoped that was the end of it.
But alas, it wasn't. At that very moment
the captain of the bandits was swearing
and kicking at the treasure heaps in the
secret cave. As soon as the cave
door had opened and he'd
seen that the pieces of
Kassim's body had gone,
he realized that somebody
else must know the secret
of the hidden cave.

"We must find whoever it is and kill him!" he roared.

"Yes, and all his family!" roared his thirty-nine men.

And so the captain and his men went into the city in disguise. They asked if there had been a recent funeral involving a corpse chopped into several pieces. They had no luck – but then one of the bandits happened to stop at the tailor's shop...

By now the tailor had had time to think about what he'd done, and he was finding it very hard to keep to his vow of secrecy.

It didn't take the bandit long to get the truth out of him, and then – after a small payment was offered and accepted – the tailor allowed himself to be blindfolded once more. He led the bandit to Ali Baba's house by touch and hearing and smell. The bandit smiled, and marked the doorpost with a small chalk cross. Then he quickly took the tailor back to his shop, and hurried off to find the captain.

A while later, Marjanah came back from shopping in the bazaar, and noticed the chalk cross. It immediately made her feel uneasy, so she found some chalk and made crosses on the other doorposts in the street. She didn't mention the incident to Ali Baba, not wanting to worry him or the rest of the family. But Marjanah decided she would definitely stay alert now.

The captain, however, wasn't so easily fooled. When he saw the crosses on every door, he marched off to the tailor's shop. Soon the happy tailor – he'd been given yet another payment of gold coins – was blindfolded again and led the captain back to Ali Baba's house. The captain didn't mark the doorpost, though – he knew he'd remember the house well enough without that...

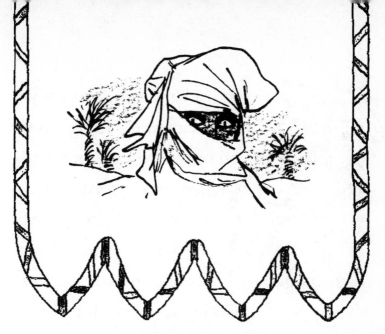

CHAPTER FOUR

MARJANAH AND THE JARS OF OLIVE OIL

THE NEXT EVENING, THERE WAS a knocking on Ali Baba's door. He opened it to a man whose face was half covered by his turban. Behind the man was a line of packhorses, each one bearing a large earthenware jar. "Good evening, friend," said the man. "I am a travelling merchant, just arrived in your city. I wondered if you might know of a place to stay."

"Why, you must stay here!" replied Ali Baba, as generous as ever, of course. "Your packhorses will be safe in our courtyard."

The man smiled wickedly as Ali Baba led him in. For he was none other than the captain in disguise. He had made inquiries about the man who lived in this house, and been told of his kindness, so he'd guessed Ali Baba would offer him a bed.

But the captain wouldn't be staying in bed. Each of those earthenware jars concealed one of the captain's men, and they were waiting for his signal – a light tap on the outside of the jar – to creep out and slaughter everyone in the house.

Marjanah prepared a meal for the guest, then went out to check that the horses were comfortable. She'd heard Ali Baba asking the merchant what was in the jars. The man had said they were filled with olive oil, but when Marjanah accidentally brushed against one of the jars, she froze when she heard a man's voice whisper from within it.

"Is it time yet?" said the voice. Suddenly Marjanah suspected that her master and his family were in mortal danger. She realised that the merchant must be the captain of the bandits, and that his men were concealed in the jars.

"Not yet," she whispered back, thinking quickly. Then she went indoors and came up with another plan.

Marjanah boiled up plenty of oil – and poured it into each of the jars, killing all thirty-nine bandits.

She went to tell Ali Baba, and just then the captain went to the courtyard to summon his men. When he realised that his plot had been uncovered he fled into the night before he too was killed. But he vowed to wreak his revenge…

Marjanah showed Ali Baba the bodies in the jars and he went cold at the thought of what might have happened.

"I can't ever thank you enough, Marjanah," Ali Baba murmured.

"I'd do anything to help you," said Marjanah. "No one has ever been as kind and generous to me as you and Ayesha!"

Things did seem to quieten down over the next few months, so Ali Baba and his family relaxed and enjoyed their prosperity.

Ali Baba even set Ahmed up in business with a shop of his own.

Then one day, several years later, Ahmed asked Ali Baba if he could invite a friend of his to dinner at their house.

"His name is Hussein," said Ahmed. "He owns the shop next door to mine."

Ali Baba agreed, and the feast was arranged. All the family were there, even Fatimah, and the guest of honour arrived bang on time.

Thoughtfully, Marjanah took Hussein's cloak to hang it up. After all this time she had begun to think that they must be safe.

But there was something about this man that made her feel uneasy.

Marjanah went round with a flask of wine. When she leaned over Hussein to pour some wine into his cup, she glimpsed something that chilled her blood – the handle of a dagger that was concealed inside Hussein's tunic.

Marjanah instantly realised why Hussein was familiar. He was disguised again, but he was obviously the merchant whose men she had killed in the jars. Which meant he was also the captain of the bandits, come to kill them all!

Marjanah slipped into the kitchen and grabbed a knife, which she kept behind her back when she returned to the feast.

She was just in time. Ali Baba had his back to Hussein and Hussein had his hand inside his tunic…

Marjanah strode over and plunged her knife into Hussein's heart. Hussein died instantly – and then there was chaos. Ayesha and Fatimah screamed – Fatimah the loudest – while both Ali Baba and Ahmed leapt to their feet with expressions of horror on their faces.

"You have killed Ahmed's friend!" wailed Ali Baba. "Have you gone mad, girl?"

"No!" said Marjanah. "He was about to kill you!"

Marjanah explained and showed Ali Baba the dagger concealed in Hussein's tunic. And when Ali Baba looked more closely at Hussein, he wondered why he hadn't seen that he was none other than the captain of the bandits...

And so, at last, they were safe. To Ali Baba's delight, Marjanah and Ahmed soon announced that they were in love and wanted to get married, which they did.

And Ali Baba and his family lived in happiness and prosperity ever after, their growing wealth helped by occasional visits to a certain hidden cave.

They were the only ones who knew about it, after all...

ALI BABA
A tale of GREED versus GOODNESS

By Tony Bradman

The story of Ali Baba comes from *The Thousand and One Nights*, the great collection of Arabic, Persian and Indian folk tales that also gave us *Aladdin* and *The Voyages of Sinbad The Sailor*. Although the original book was put together in the Middle Ages in Baghdad and Cairo, it was translated from Arabic into French, English and other languages in the eighteenth and nineteenth centuries and continues to be popular the world over today.

And no story is better known and loved than that of the humble woodcutter who stumbles on a cave of stolen treasure. The tale of Ali Baba has everything that makes *The Thousand and One Nights* a joy to read – a wildly inventive plot, a touch of magic, a wide range of fascinating characters, terrific suspense, surprises and comedy. It's also quite a violent tale, but violence was more common in the days when this story was first told, and it's the bad characters who suffer most.

In fact, there's even more to Ali Baba's story. Like many great folk tales, it has a very strong moral. Ali Baba is poor and weak and has no one but his wife and son to help him. So how can he hope to succeed against his rich brother Kassim, and forty strong, violent thieves?

The answer is simple – Ali Baba is a good person, and goodness is usually rewarded in folk tales and legends all over the world. In the Greek tale of Jason and his fellow Argonauts, for example, Jason's quest is failing until he does a king a good turn and is helped on his way once more. In European myths about fishermen and mermaids, the fishermen who are kind to the mermaids they catch in their nets by mistake are always the ones the mermaids help in times of need.

Ali Baba's family are saved by Marjanah, a servant girl who loves them because they're kind to her. The villains help bring about their own downfall because they're so greedy – but Marjanah also has to be very resourceful. So the moral of the story is goodness wins every time – especially if you're clever and brave too!

47

ORCHARD MYTHS AND CLASSICS

THE GREATEST ADVENTURES IN THE WORLD

TONY BRADMAN & TONY ROSS

Ali Baba and the Stolen Treasure	1 84362 473 7
Jason and the Voyage to the Edge of the World	1 84362 472 9
Robin Hood and the Silver Arrow	1 84362 474 5
Aladdin and the Fabulous Genie	1 84362 477 X
Arthur and the King's Sword	1 84362 475 3
William Tell and the Apple for Freedom	1 84362 476 1

All priced at £3.99